The Lord in the Lake in Limerick

D0231417

Oisín McGann
Illustrated by **Derry Dillon**

MAC
MYTHICAL ACTIVITY CONTROL

Published 2014
Poolbeg Press Ltd

123 Grange Hill, Baldoyle
Dublin 13, Ireland

Text © Poolbeg Press Ltd 2014

A catalogue record for this book is available from the British Library.

ISBN 978 1 78199 975 2

Cover design and illustrations by Derry Dillon
Printed by GPS Colour Graphics Ltd, Alexander Road, Belfast BT6 9HP

The Lord in the Lake in Limerick

This book belongs to

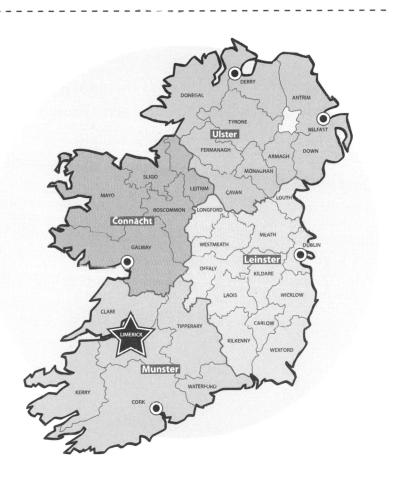

MAC – Mythical Activity Control

Mission Info

There was a time, long ago, when Ireland was a place of magic. Now, all the magical people and creatures live in the Otherworld. To people like you, they are just myths and legends. But sometimes they can escape into your world.

Mythical Activity Control guards the doorways to your world. And when someone gets through, it's MAC's job to bring them back.

From the Agent Files:

ÁINE *(pronounced 'AWN-yeh')*
Ancestor:
Áine, Goddess of
Summer and Light.
Personality:
Smart but stubborn.
Loves nature.
Can judge the moods of
people and animals.
Power:
Can talk to animals.
Can travel through
mirrors and polished metal.

FIONN *(pronounced 'Fy-UNN')*
Ancestor:
Legendary warrior Fionn McCool.
Personality:
Clever, sensible, but curious too
and that can get him into trouble.
Power:
Can connect to information from
either world by biting his thumb,
like his ancestor after he tasted
the Salmon of Knowledge.
Can travel through mirrors and polished metal.

TOGETHER, they help keep you safe from the
wild magic of the Otherworld.

Also in the MAC series

Viking Thunder in Dublin
The Banshee Queen of Cork
Queen Maebh's Raging Return to Galway

ALSO...

There are ten white feathers hidden in this adventure. Can you find them?

It was just after dawn when the dripping head rose out of the waters of Lough Gur. A young man and woman were walking beside the pretty lake in County Limerick. They were taking pictures when they spotted the head and stopped in surprise. They saw a man wearing scuba gear stand up out of the water.

They snapped a few shots as he waded to shore.

He was in a hurry and he was holding a bag in his hand. Water dripped from his bristly red hair as he pulled off his flippers and rushed over to his van. He tugged off his mask and his oxygen tank. Throwing them into the back of the van with his flippers, he looked over at the lake. There was fear on his face. But then he looked at the bag in his hands and his face broke into a nasty smile.

Without even bothering to dry himself, he jumped into the driver's seat. Starting the van, he revved the engine. He drove straight at the young couple and they yelped as they jumped out of his way. He charged past, racing out of the car park and onto the road.

"Watch where you're going, you eejit!" the young man roared.

Out in the lake, a strange light glowed deep in the water. The surface began to bubble and churn. In an explosion of spray, a man burst from the water on the back of a dappled grey horse. The man was dressed in fancy, old-fashioned clothes. Like a lord from medieval times.

The couple watched in shock as the horse galloped across the surface of the water. Then they started taking photos of this too.

"Which way did the thief go?" the rider demanded as he came to a stop in front of them.

They stared up at him, so stunned they were unable to speak.

"WHERE DID HE GO?" he bellowed at them.

The woman pointed a finger up the road. The horseman growled and tapped his heels into the horse's sides. Horse and rider took off at incredible speed, faster than any animal should be able to travel.

A few minutes after the mysterious rider burst from the water, two more figures appeared. A boy and a girl, they rose from the same place in the water as the rider. In the water beneath them was a gate to the Otherworld which they had just come through. But they had to swim to shore. Their clothes dried magically as they stood looking around.

Their names were Áine and Fionn. They were secret agents. They worked for MAC – Mythical Activity Control. When someone escaped from the Otherworld into this world, it was Áine and Fionn's job to bring them back.

The two photographers were still there. Fionn walked up to them.

"Excuse me," he said. "Could I see your cameras for a second?"

The couple were so amazed at the appearance of these two kids that they just handed the cameras over. Fionn pressed his thumb against the side of each camera.

"Thanks," he said, giving them back.

He stuck his thumb in his mouth and bit it thoughtfully. He had the power to connect to the web by doing this, or pull down knowledge from the Otherworld. And, in his mind, he could look through the photos his thumb had taken off the cameras.

"Yeah, it was Gearóid Iarla all right," he said to Áine. "He came out of the lake on that horse of his."

"What's going on?" she wondered aloud.

She knew Gearóid quite well. He had been friends with her own ancestor, the Goddess Áine, and had kept in touch with the family ever since. She gazed at the hoofprints on the grass in front of her.

"Gearóid Iarla is nearly 700 years old. He was the lord of this land once. A very powerful man. Now, he's supposed to sleep at the bottom of this lake, by the gate to the Otherworld. And he's only allowed ride out when the land is threatened. And it's not. Looking at these hoofprints, I'd say he was in a hurry."

"Someone came out of the lake ahead of him," Fionn said, his thumb still in his mouth as he studied the pictures in his head. "The guy got into a van and drove away. The sign on the side of the van reads: 'Ballyhoura Adventure Tours'. Ballyhoura's a range of mountains south of here. Maybe we should start looking there."

"It won't be easy catching Gearóid Iarla," Áine said. "His horse, Luas, has magic silver horseshoes and it's really fast."

"That's true," Fionn said. "But we do have the mirrors."

They both turned and hurried towards the Lough Gur Visitors' Centre. The doors were locked, but the two MAC agents were good at picking locks. They disappeared inside. When the man and woman checked their cameras, they found their photos had been wiped. And then their batteries went dead.

When you're dealing with legends from the Otherworld, you have to be able to move fast. Áine and Fionn had the power to travel instantly through mirrors. They could jump in through a mirror in one place and out through another somewhere else. The mirrors were magical doorways. They could also jump through polished metal.

This meant they could move pretty fast,
which is useful if you have to catch a man riding
a magical horse. From the Visitor's Centre in
Lough Gur, they found their way to a mirror
in the office of Ballyhoura Adventure Tours.
But when they leapt out, there was no sign of
Gearóid Iarla or the man he was chasing.

As Fionn searched the office for clues, Áine went outside. The building had a shed with kayaks, bicycles and gear for other outdoor activities. The place was set in a clearing surrounded by forest and mountains.

Áine found a squirrel in a tree and waved up to it.

"Hello!" she said. "Can you tell me anything about the man who works here?"

This was her magical power. She could talk to animals. The squirrel was excited and talked very fast. It kept offering Áine nuts, but it was able to tell her a lot too.

Fionn walked outside. He wasn't so good with animals.

Áine said goodbye to the squirrel as it scampered away.

"The man's name is Fox," she told her partner. "None of the animals like him. He's a thief. Mostly, he steals magical objects."

"He's also a huge fan of Munster rugby," Fionn told her. He held up a diary. "And he's got a meeting with the managers at Thomond Park in Limerick today. I think he's trying to sell them something."

"He must have stolen something from Gearoid," Áine muttered. "But what? And why try and sell it to a rugby team?"

"Only one way to find out," Fionn said. "Let's catch him and ask him."

The two MAC agents jumped out of a mirror in one of the dressing rooms of the huge rugby stadium. They heard the faint sound of a man screaming for help. Sprinting down the passage, they made their way up the tunnel where the players come out at the start of a match.

Looking out, Áine and Fionn saw a man with bristly red hair running at full speed across the grass towards them. Up on the stand on the far side of the pitch, Gearóid Iarla was riding down the steps on his horse. He jumped Luas right over the fence and started galloping across the pitch.

Fox saw the MAC agents and turned away, clambering up over the seats to one side. Áine wanted to stop Fox, but that wasn't their job. They were here for Gearóid Iarla.

"MAC agents!" Fionn shouted, waving his badge at the rider. He jumped in front of Luas who reared up in front of him. Fionn didn't flinch. "Stop right there! Gearóid, you left the Otherworld without permission! We're here to take you back!"

"Catch him!" Gearóid shouted back, pointing at Fox. The thief was disappearing down a tunnel. "That rotter stole two of Luas's shoes while I was sleeping!"

Now Áine understood.

"Fionn, we have to help him!" she said. "Luas's shoes are made of enchanted silver. Gearóid is one of the guardians of Ireland. When he rides into battle, those horseshoes have the power to summon an army of warriors to ride with him!"

"That's why Fox wanted to sell a pair of horseshoes to the Munster rugby team," Fionn groaned. "To give them an army of warriors to defeat their enemies."

"The Munster team said no, they didn't want them," Gearóid grunted. "It would be cheating."

"Besides, I've seen them play," Fionn said. "They don't need an army to beat anyone."

"Okay," Áine sighed. "But now Fox will try to sell the shoes somewhere else. Or try and use them himself. We have to get those silver horseshoes back before he figures out how to summon an army who will obey his every command."

Áine and Fionn jumped on the horse behind Gearóid Iarla. They rode past the shocked security guards at the gate and out of the stadium. Fox dived into his van and drove off, tyres screeching. Gearóid gave chase, but his horse was growing tired. With two of its magic shoes missing, it couldn't run at this speed for long.

They came to the bank of the River Shannon. Fox was well ahead. He turned right onto the road by the river. They followed him, racing down past the famous Treaty Stone. Luas whickered angrily and Áine listened.

"She says Fox stole the silver shoes while she was sleeping," Áine told them. "He used a magic pincers to pull them off. She's very embarrassed about it. She only woke up as he was escaping."

"So where did he find magic pincers?" Fionn asked. "Hang on."

He bit his thumb and information from the web flowed into his mind.

"A pair of antique pincers was stolen from the Hunt Museum last week," he said. "Maybe he's going back there, to find a tool that will make the shoes work for him!"

"The museum's right there," Áine said, pointing. "On the other side of the river!"

"Hold on tight!" Gearóid roared.

He turned the horse, jumping her right over the wall between them and the wide river. Áine and Fionn clung on as Luas galloped across the surface of the water. Fox had to take a longer way around, across a bridge, so they reached the museum before him. He growled as he saw them and went speeding past. They took off after him, but Luas was panting for breath and slowing down.

"He must not reach King John's Castle!" Gearóid shouted. "The ghosts of old soldiers sleep there. If he takes those shoes through the gate, he'll wake up those ghosts!"

Áine called out to a flock of crows up on the walls of the castle. The big black birds let out loud caws in answer. They swooped down on Fox as he jumped out of his car. They flapped around him, getting in his way as he tried to reach the castle gate.

Luas galloped up and Fionn leapt off, knocking Fox flat on his back. Áine dropped down and grabbed the bag of horseshoes. She thanked the crows as they returned to the castle walls.

"What are you going to do?" Fox asked as Fionn held him in an armlock. "Will you put me in some strange Otherworld prison?"

"We don't have much use for prisons," Áine replied, taking the pair of horseshoes from the bag. "We do things a little differently. You wanted these shoes . . . well, now you have them."

She held them against Fox's feet. They stuck and, with a flash of light, his feet turned into hooves. He let out a scared yelp.

"Don't worry," Áine told him. "The shoes will return to Gearóid and your feet will change back. All you have to do is walk the length of the Shannon, to where the river starts in County Cavan. And you can only walk."

"But the river's over three hundred kilometres long!" Fox whined.

"Better get started then," Fionn told him as he let him go.

Fox looked at the two MAC agents and then at Gearóid Iarla. They weren't joking. With a sulky sigh, he turned around and started up the road along the river.

"Ha!" Gearóid chuckled. "I believe it is a very pretty walk. But Luas is tired. I think it's time for me to go back to bed and await the return of my horse's shoes."

"What's it like, sleeping by a gate at the bottom of a lake?" Fionn asked.

"Quiet," Gearóid replied. "Farewell, my friends. It was good to feel the thrill of the chase once more, but this was not my time to rise. Goodbye!"

And with that, he snapped his reins and galloped away. Áine and Fionn watched as he and his horse took off across the city, headed back towards Lough Gur. Turning back, the two agents saw Fox slowly making his way up the river.

"And people say horseshoes are lucky," Fionn sighed.

"Fox was lucky," Áine said. "He was lucky we caught him before Gearóid did. So, what do you fancy doing now?"

"How about a stroll along the Shannon?" Fionn suggested. "I hear it's a pretty walk . . . when you don't have to march all the way to Cavan in horseshoes!"

"All right then," Áine said, smiling. "Let's take a walk."

And so they did.

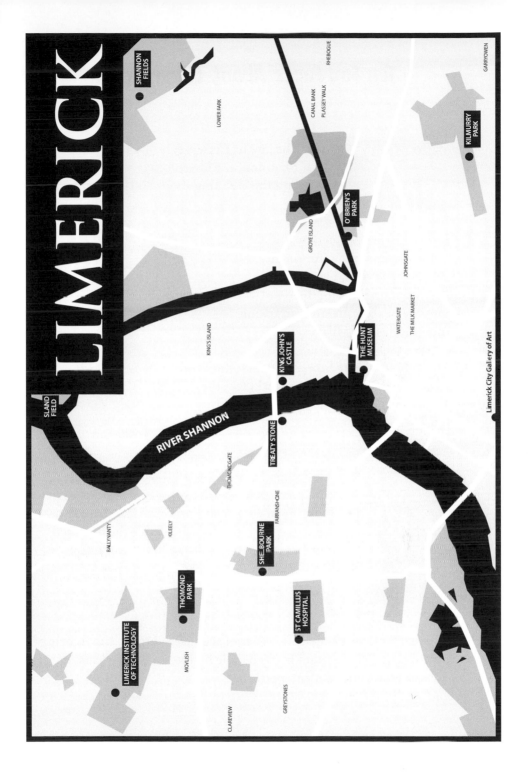

Ten Fun Facts About Limerick!

1. The city of Limerick is on the River Shannon, the longest river in Ireland and the UK. It is about 360 kilometres long.

2. Limerick was founded by the Vikings who built a fort on an island in the river. From there they went on raids up the river into the heart of Ireland, attacking monasteries and villages.

3. The famous Treaty Stone on which the Treaty of Limerick was signed, in 1691 after the Williamite War, was actually a mounting block for mounting horses.

4. 'Galloping Hogan' was a 'rapparee' (guerrilla fighter) who guided the cavalry from Limerick in 1690 to blow up an enemy siege train. After the war he became one of the 'Wild Geese'– the defeated soldiers who left Ireland to join armies all over the world.

5. The year 1739 was called 'The Year of the Great Frost'. The freezing period lasted 40 days and many people had to survive on 'cats, dogs, mice, carrion, putrid meat, nettles'.

6. In 1868 the 'Ardagh Hoard' was found by two boys digging in a potato field in County Limerick. It included a decorated silver chalice and was made up of 354 separate pieces.

7. In 1892, after £35,000 was spent on new water pipes for Limerick city, when the taps were turned on eels from the river came through them into the kitchens!

8. A 'limerick' is a 5-line nonsense poem, rhyming in a special way, with special lengths to the lines, usually mentioning a place in the first line. Here is one:

There was an old man of Nantucket
Who kept all his cash in a bucket;
But his daughter, named Nan,
Ran away with a man,
And as for the bucket, Nan-took-it.

Write your own limerick!

9. Limerick is famous for its love of rugby. Garryowen, a Limerick team, gave its name to a special kind of 'up-and-under' kick where the ball is kicked very high to allow the kicking team to get under it before it comes down.

10. Limerick is the only place where 'runners' or 'trainers' are called 'tackies' – except for South Africa! It may be that British troops, after the Boer War, brought this word for sports shoes back with them to Limerick!

If you enjoyed this book from
Poolbeg why not visit our website:

www.poolbeg.com

and get another book delivered straight
to your home or to a friend's home.

All books despatched within 24 hours.

POOLBEG

Why not join our mailing list
at www.poolbeg.com and get some
fantastic offers, competitions,
author interviews and much more?

@PoolbegBooks